# ASTON MARTIN DB9

BY EMILY ROSE OACHS

BELLWETHER MEDIA • MINNEAPOLIS, MN

Are you ready to take it to the extreme? Torque books thrust you into the action-packed world of sports, vehicles, mystery, and adventure. These books may include dirt, smoke, fire, and dangerous stunts.

**WARNING**: read at your own risk.

This edition first published in 2017 by Bellwether Media, Inc.

No part of this publication may be reproduced in whole or in part without written permission of the publisher. For information regarding permission, write to Bellwether Media, Inc., Attention: Permissions Department, 5357 Penn Avenue South, Minneapolis, MN 55419.

Library of Congress Cataloging-in-Publication Data

Names: Oachs, Emily Rose, author.
Title: Aston Martin DB9 / by Emily Rose Oachs.
Other titles: Car Crazy (Minneapolis, Minn.)
Description: Minneapolis, MN : Bellwether Media, Inc., 2017. | Series: Torque: Car Crazy | Audience: Ages 7-12. | Includes bibliographical references and index.
Identifiers: LCCN 2016033349 (print) | LCCN 2016041183 (ebook) | ISBN 9781626175754 (hardcover : alk. paper) | ISBN 9781681033044 (ebook)
Subjects: LCSH: Aston Martin DB9 automobile–Juvenile literature.
Classification: LCC TL215.A75 O23 2017 (print) | LCC TL215.A75 (ebook) | DDC 629.222/2–dc23
LC record available at https://lccn.loc.gov/2016033349

Text copyright © 2017 by Bellwether Media, Inc. TORQUE and associated logos are trademarks and/or registered trademarks of Bellwether Media, Inc. SCHOLASTIC, CHILDREN'S PRESS, and associated logos are trademarks and/or registered trademarks of Scholastic Inc.

Editor: Betsy Rathburn   Designer: Brittany McIntosh

Printed in the United States of America, North Mankato, MN.

# TABLE OF CONTENTS

| | |
|---|---|
| Head-Turning Style | 4 |
| The History of Aston Martin | 8 |
| Aston Martin DB9 | 12 |
| Technology and Gear | 14 |
| Today and the Future | 20 |
| Glossary | 22 |
| To Learn More | 23 |
| Index | 24 |

# HEAD-TURNING STYLE

A crowd gathers around a parked Aston Martin DB9. The people admire the graceful curves and stylish details of the **supercar**. The driver walks up and slides into the car. He pushes the key into place. The engine roars to life, and the driver steps on the gas.

The DB9 zooms forward. Within 5 seconds, it reaches 60 miles (96.6 kilometers) per hour. The car speeds even faster down a curvy road. It handles the turns easily. The DB9 has style and power!

# THE HISTORY OF ASTON MARTIN

**1914 Aston Hill Climb**

In 1913, Robert Bamford and Lionel Martin formed a new car company. The pair wanted to build cars that were beautiful and fast. The company was named Aston Martin after Lionel completed the Aston Hill Climb in 1914.

Aston Martin found early racing success. The company began competing in the **24 Hours of Le Mans** race in 1928. In the 1932 and 1933 races, Aston Martin cars finished at the top of their class. During this time, the company continued to make more cars each year.

1934
Aston Martin Ulster

after, the company introduced its famous DB line. A DB5 appeared in the 1964 James Bond film *Goldfinger*. This boosted the company's sales and fame.

1964 Aston Martin DB5 in *Goldfinger*

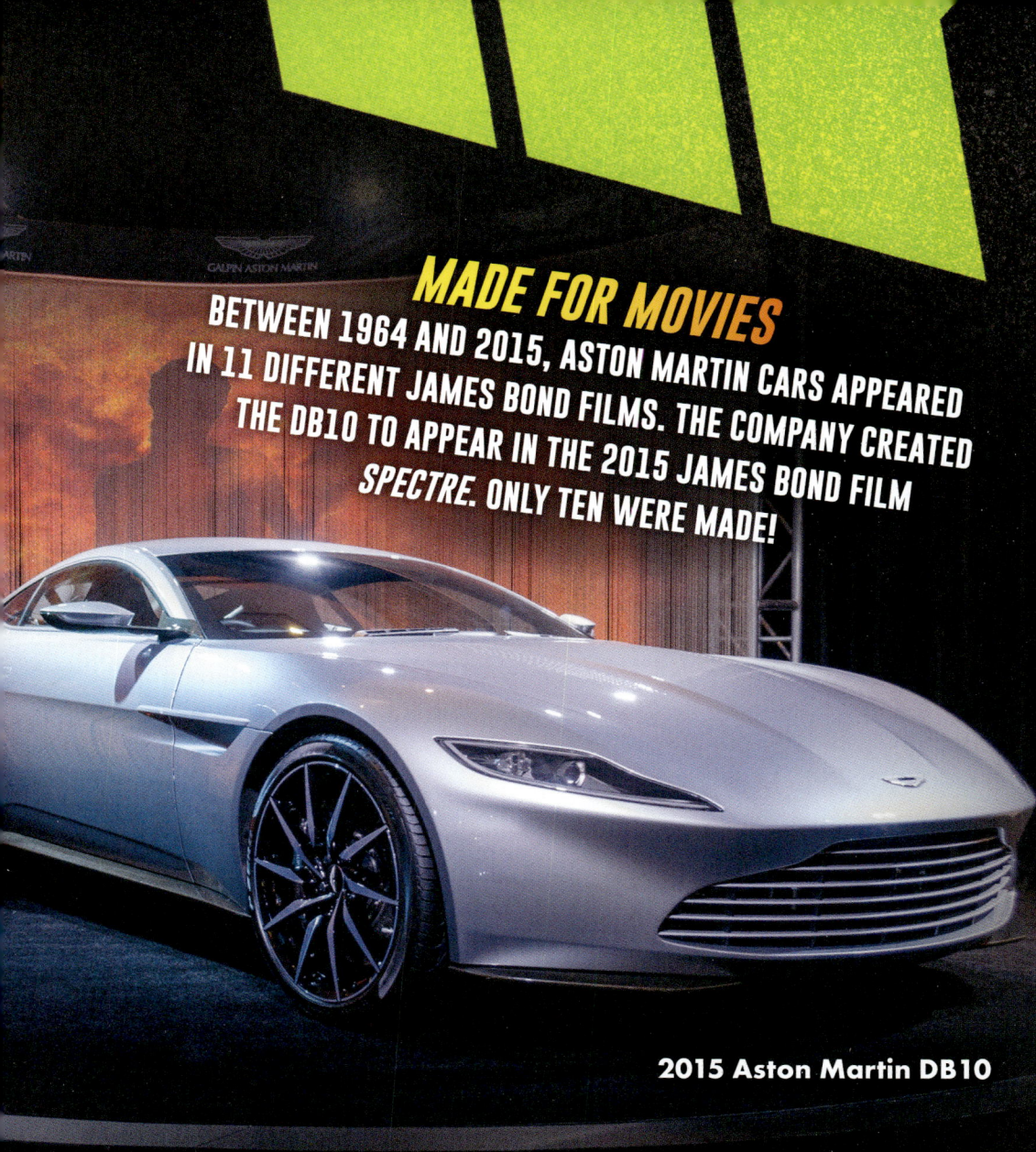

## MADE FOR MOVIES
BETWEEN 1964 AND 2015, ASTON MARTIN CARS APPEARED IN 11 DIFFERENT JAMES BOND FILMS. THE COMPANY CREATED THE DB10 TO APPEAR IN THE 2015 JAMES BOND FILM SPECTRE. ONLY TEN WERE MADE!

2015 Aston Martin DB10

Since then, Aston Martin has continued to produce popular **luxury** cars. Fans can still see them on roads, racetracks, and movie screens today!

# ASTON MARTIN DB9

Aston Martin first introduced the DB9 in 2003. It took the place of the DB7 in the company's lineup. Like earlier DBs, the DB9 boasts comfort and style. But this **model** brings even better performance to the DB line. It comes as both a **coupe** and a **convertible**.

**convertible**

**coupe**

# READY TO WRITE
THE DB9 HAS MANY SPECIAL FEATURES. SOME COME WITH A BUILT-IN PEN!

**2003 Aston Martin DB9**

# TECHNOLOGY AND GEAR

Smooth lines give the DB9's body a stylish, **aerodynamic** shape. **Strakes** at the sides and a small **spoiler** at the rear help air pass easily over the car.

The frame and most of the body are **aluminum**. This makes the DB9 light and strong. To balance the car, the engine sits low to the ground.

strake

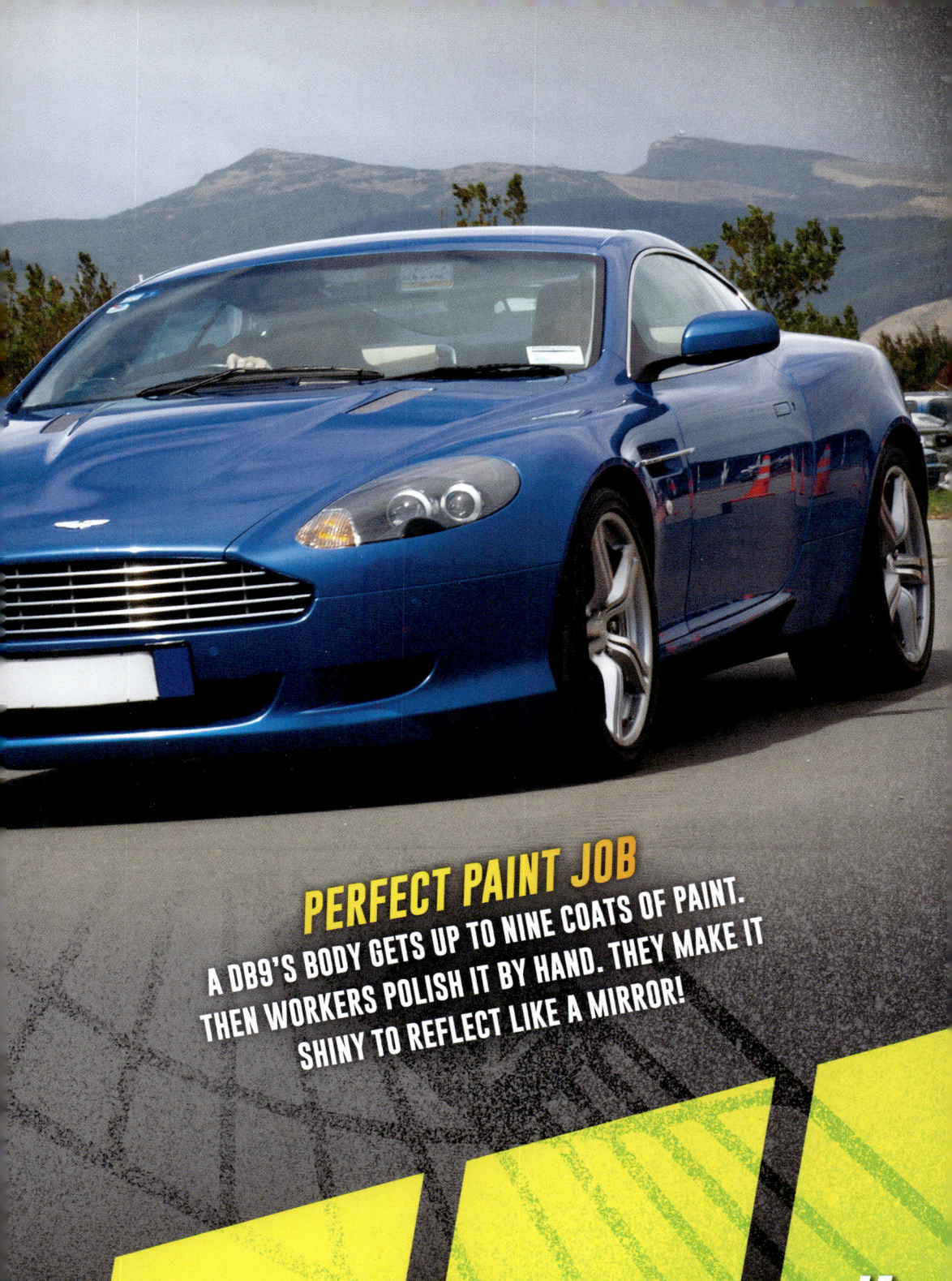

## PERFECT PAINT JOB

A DB9'S BODY GETS UP TO NINE COATS OF PAINT. THEN WORKERS POLISH IT BY HAND. THEY MAKE IT SHINY TO REFLECT LIKE A MIRROR!

V12 engine

Inside, the DB9 is sleek and comfortable. The hand-sewn leather steering wheel and seats give the car a classy feel. A small screen flips up to give driving directions. Polished glass buttons sit at the driver's fingertips on the dashboard. With the push of a button, the **V12 engine** comes to life.

paddle shifter

On the steering wheel, **paddle shifters** allow drivers to change gears by hand. For more power and better **handling**, a driver can switch to the sport driving mode.

Three different settings in the DB9's **suspension system** also give drivers improved control. Drivers can change these settings to best fit road conditions.

# 2015 ASTON MARTIN DB9 SPECIFICATIONS

| | |
|---|---|
| CAR STYLE | COUPE OR CONVERTIBLE |
| ENGINE | 6.0L V12 |
| TOP SPEED | 183 MILES (295 KILOMETERS) PER HOUR |
| 0 - 60 TIME | 4.5 SECONDS |
| HORSEPOWER | 510 HP (380 KILOWATTS) @ 6,500 RPM |
| CURB WEIGHT (COUPE) | 3,935 POUNDS (1,785 KILOGRAMS) |
| (CONVERTIBLE) | 4,167 POUNDS (1,890 KILOGRAMS) |
| WIDTH | 81.1 INCHES (206.1 CENTIMETERS) |
| LENGTH | 185.8 INCHES (472 CENTIMETERS) |
| HEIGHT | 50.5 INCHES (128.2 CENTIMETERS) |
| WHEEL SIZE | 20 INCHES (51 CENTIMETERS) |
| COST | STARTS AROUND $200,000 |

# TODAY AND THE FUTURE

Drivers love how the Aston Martin DB9 blends speed and comfort. The company improved these features and introduced the DB11 in 2016. The new model is the next to carry on the DB line's history of luxury and power!

# HOW TO SPOT AN ASTON MARTIN DB9

**SMOOTH BODY LINES**

**SPOILER**

**SIDE STRAKES**

Aston Martin DB11

# GLOSSARY

**24 Hours of Le Mans**—a race in which a team of drivers competes for 24 hours

**aerodynamic**—having a shape that can move through the air quickly

**aluminum**—a strong, lightweight metal

**convertible**—a car with a folding or soft roof

**coupe**—a car with a hard roof and two doors

**handling**—how a car performs around turns

**luxury**—expensive and offering great comfort

**model**—a specific kind of car

**paddle shifters**—paddles on the steering wheel of a car that allow a driver to change gears

**spoiler**—a part on the back of a car that helps the car grip the road

**strakes**—folds in the sides of a car's body

**supercar**—an expensive and high-performing sports car

**suspension system**—a series of springs and shocks that help a car grip the road

**V12 engine**—an engine with 12 cylinders arranged in the shape of a "V"

# TO LEARN MORE

## AT THE LIBRARY

Colson, Rob. *Aston Martin*. New York, N.Y.: PowerKids Press, 2011.

Gifford, Clive. *Car Crazy*. New York, N.Y.: D.K. Publishing, 2012.

Gray, Leon. *Fast and Cool Cars.* New York, N.Y.: DK, Penguin Random House, 2015.

## ON THE WEB

Learning more about the Aston Martin DB9 is as easy as 1, 2, 3.

1. Go to www.factsurfer.com.

2. Enter "Aston Martin DB9" into the search box.

3. Click the "Surf" button and you will see a list of related web sites.

With factsurfer.com, finding more information is just a click away.

# INDEX

24 Hours of Le Mans, 9
acceleration, 6
aerodynamic, 14
Aston Hill Climb, 8
Bamford, Robert, 8
body, 12, 14, 15, 21
Bond, James, 10, 11
Brown, David, 10
comfort, 12, 17, 20
company, 8, 9, 10, 11, 20
DB line, 10, 11, 12, 20, 21
drive settings, 18
engine, 5, 14, 16, 17
*Goldfinger*, 10
handling, 6, 18

history, 8, 9, 10, 11, 12, 20
how to spot, 21
interior, 13, 17, 18
Martin, Lionel, 8
models, 9, 10, 11, 12, 20, 21
name, 8
paddle shifters, 18
racing, 9
specifications, 19
*Spectre*, 11
speed, 6, 20
spoiler, 14, 21
strakes, 14, 21
suspension system, 18

The images in this book are reproduced through the courtesy of: totojang1977, front cover; Cernan Elias/ Alamy, pp. 4-5; Transtock/ SuperStock, pp. 6-7, 16 (top), 18; Hulton Archive/ Stringer/ Getty Images, p. 8; picture alliance/ J.W.Alker/ Newscom, p. 9; BFA/ United Artists/ Alamy, p. 10; betto rodrigues, p. 11; Drive Images/ Alamy, p. 12 (top); ben smith, pp. 12 (bottom), 21 (top left, top right); culture-images GmbH/ Alamy, p. 13; Quentin Bargate/ Alamy, p. 14; falun, p. 15; Simon Stuart-Miller/ Alamy, p. 16 (bottom); Sjoerd van der Wal, p. 17; Andrey Troitskiy, p. 19; Max Earey, pp. 20-21; VanderWolf Images, p. 21 (top center); sippakorn, p. 21 (bottom).